W9-AHH-172

JUNGLE GYM JITTERS
CHUCK RICHARDS
WALKER & COMPANY
NEW YORK

To my parents, Ken and Helen Richards, for the encouragement they gave me as a young artist—and to my wife, Diana, and kids, Andy and Kim, for their continued love and support. —C. R.

First published in the United States of America in 2004 by
Walker Publishing Company, Inc.

Published simultaneously in Canada by Fitzhenry and Whiteside,
Markham, Ontario L3R 4T8

For information about permission to reproduce selections from this book, write to Permissions, Walker & Company, 104 Fifth Avenue, New York, New York 10011

Library of Congress Cataloging-in-Publication Data

Richards, Chuck, 1957-
Jungle gym jitters / Chuck Richards.
p. cm.
Summary: Jerry's imaginative dad likes to build things, but when the jungle gym that started out fun grows out of control, Jerry's fear of heights—and the zoo animals and mobs of people the gym attracts—give Jerry the jitters.
ISBN 0-8027-8931-5 — ISBN 0-8027-8932-3
[1. Playgrounds—Fiction. 2. Fear—Fiction. 3. Building—Fiction. 4. Zoo animals—Fiction. 5. Humorous stories. 6. Stories in rhyme.] I. Title.

PZ8.3.R3795Ju 2004
[E]—dc22
2004049488

The artist used colored pencils and graphite pencil on warm gray paper to create the illustrations for this book.

Book design by Nicole Gastonguay

Visit Walker & Company's Web site at www.walkeryoungreaders.com

Printed in the United States of America

2 4 6 8 10 9 7 5 3

Jerry J. Jingle had fun every day,
for Jerry's dad, George, had a brain made for play.
When Dad got an idea that planted its seed,
fun would sprout up like a blossoming weed.

Now Jerry's mom, Midge, had been bugging his pop
to clear out the "jungle of junk" in his shop.
But Dad was distracted by silly squirrel pranks
and got an idea for his stack of wood planks.

By late afternoon Dad had proudly unveiled
the new jungle gym his hammer just nailed.
Jerry hung loose with a monkey-faced frown
while Judy, his sister, showed off upside down.

That night after supper, as Jerry did math
and Judy went up for her usual bath,
nobody saw that while washing the dishes,
Dad began planning his jungle gym wishes.

At dawn the next day, Jerry jumped out of bed
to a hammer that *TAP-TAPPA-TAPPED* in his head.
His eyes grew in size at the overgrown sight
of the jungle gym Dad had now tripled in height.

Monday at work found George overreacting
to playful ideas that became too distracting.
As one might have guessed, the boss wasn't impressed,
so he sent Dad home early to catch up on rest.

When Jerry came home his mouth opened in awe.
His friends were sky-high on a giant seesaw.
As he studied the moves of those strange seesaw sitters
he was suddenly sick with the jungle gym jitters!

Sparky's
Electrical
Supply
DONUT CITY
Times
B-B-Q
Menu

While dunking a donut the following morning,
a vision of fun came to Dad without warning.
And Jerry could tell by the way he was looking
that this meant more jungle gym trouble was cooking.

Long strings of tire swings swooped up through the sky
as, longingly, Jerry watched life pass him by.
A contest for "king of the jungle" took place.
Of course, Judy won with her usual grace.

Who would have thought that just washing the car
could make his dad act in a way this bizarre?
Jerry ducked clear of the garden hose stream.
To him this was all one big, terrible dream.

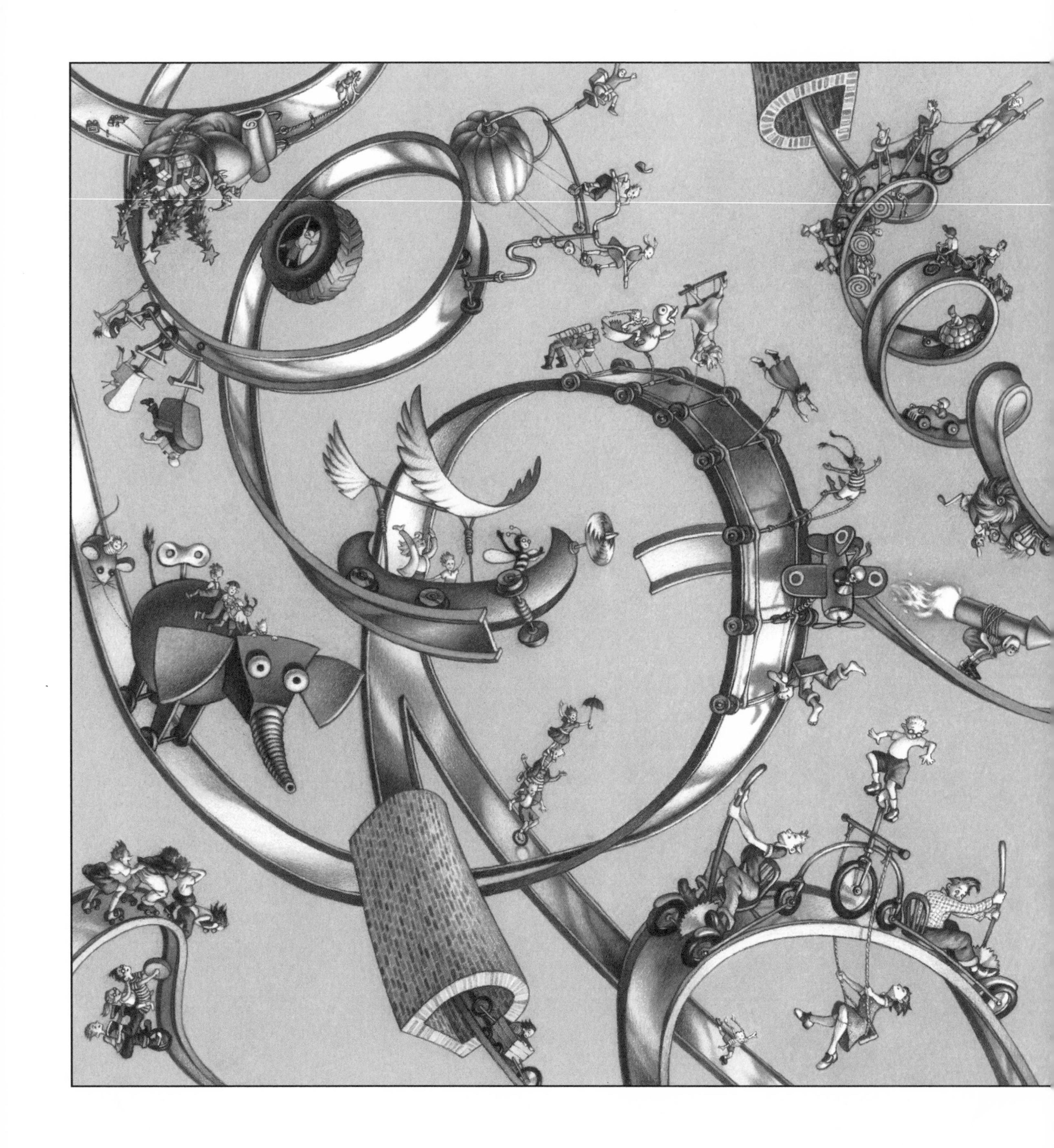

But Jerry's worst nightmares would soon be outmatched
by the tangle of tracks and long tunnels that scratched
at the summery sky like some scribbly scrawl,
with silvery loops that were sixty feet tall.

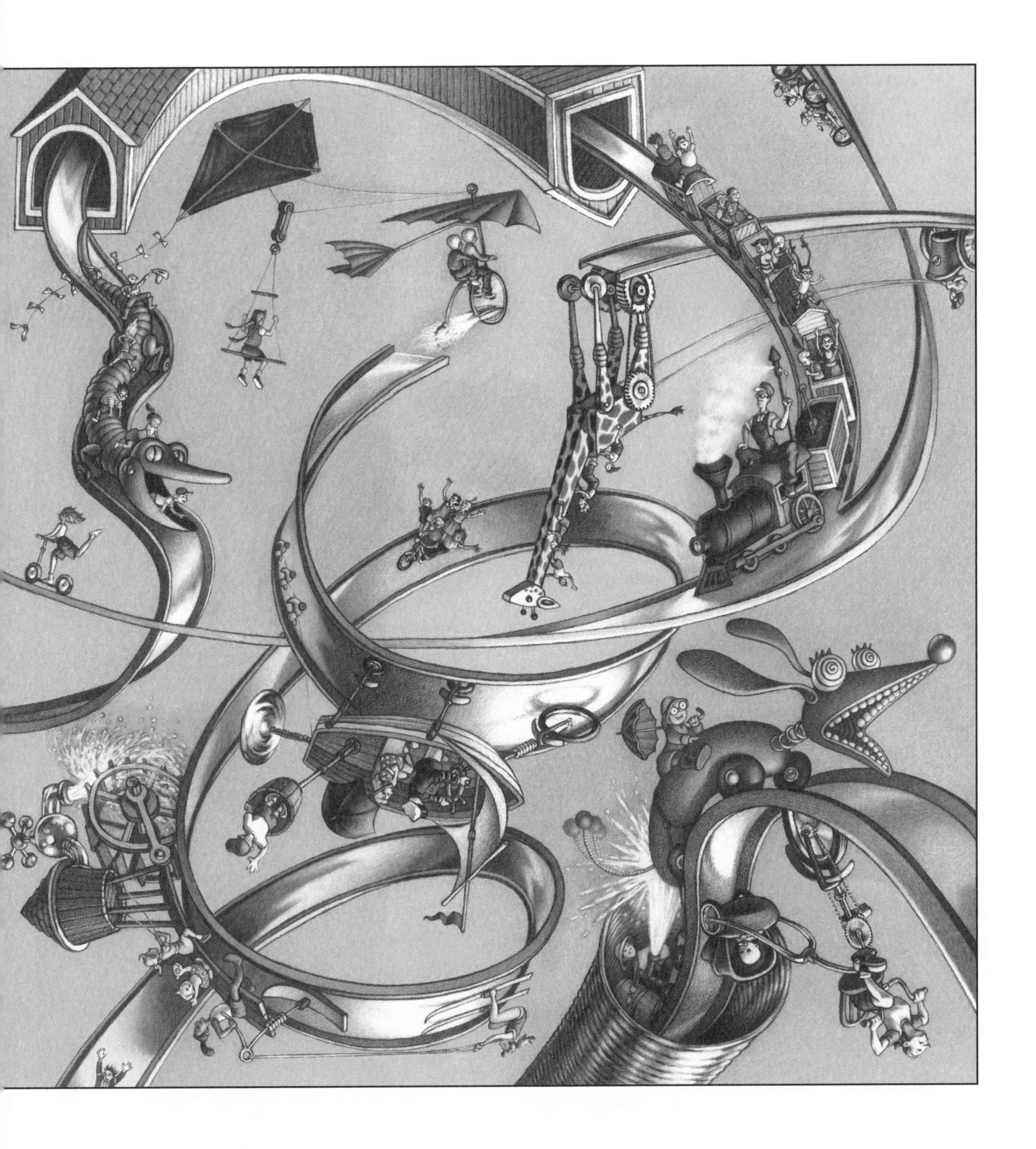

His knees started knocking, his tongue started swelling.
Jerry once lost his lunch (but that's not worth telling).
The poor boy knew this of his terrible curse:
his jungle gym jitters would only get worse.

In a couple of days this prediction came true.
Dad went off on "safari" (a trip to the zoo)
and brought back a truckload of jungly critters,
whose animal antics gave Jerry worse jitters.

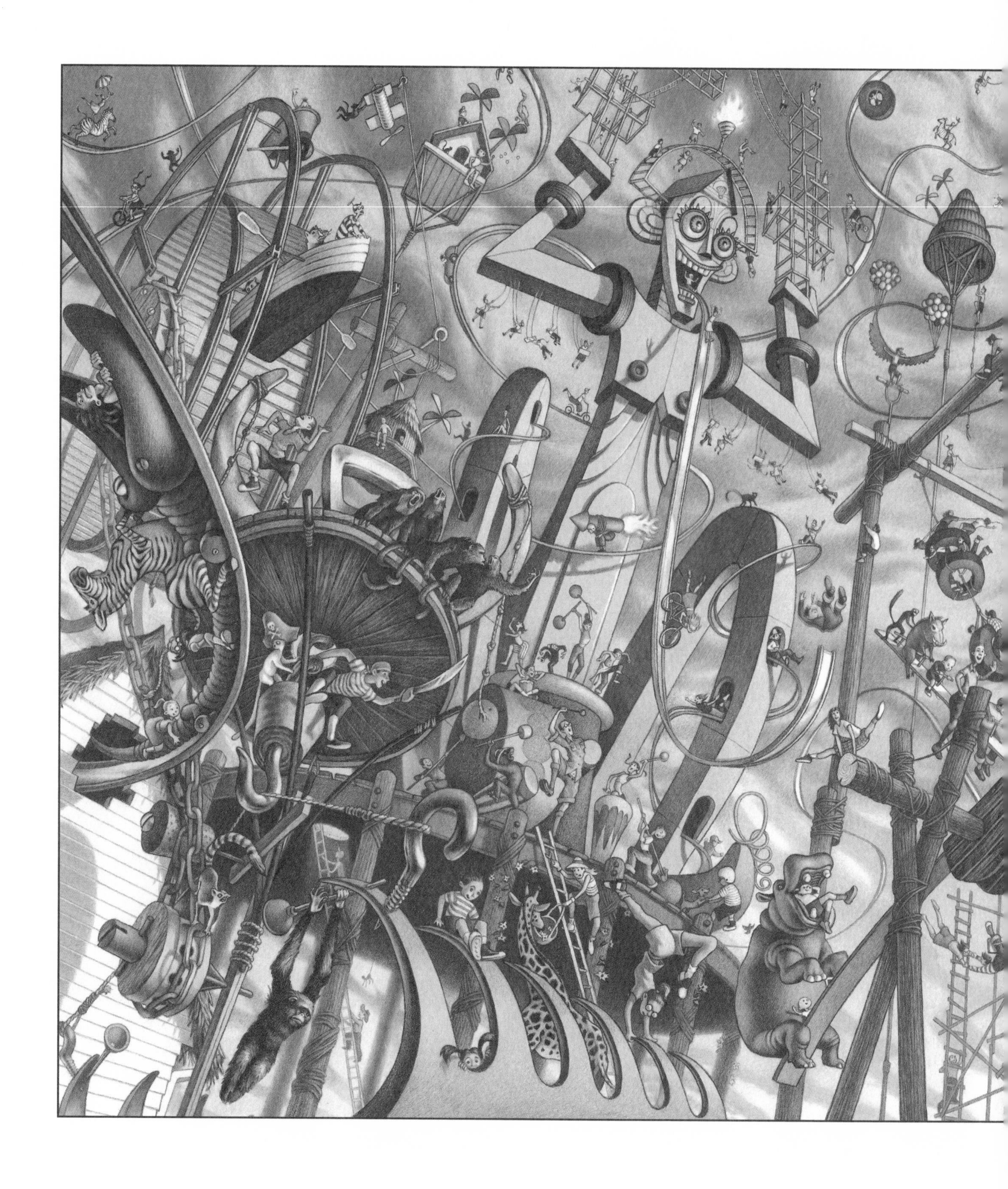

The garage was demolished, and where it once stood
was a towering giant of tires and wood.
And animal acrobats swung through the sky,
while daredevil kids made up new ways to fly.

Now Jerry's heart thumped, and his ears started ringing.
He hardly could stand all this swooping and swinging.
To make matters worse, Jerry's house was a mess,
and living there caused more emotional stress. . . .

For Dad had cut tunnels that ran through the place.
The coaster now *WHOOSHED* through their living room space.
But worse than the noise in this upside-down dwelling
were animal houseguests you couldn't help smelling!

Not seeing his family's growing frustration,
Dad proudly made plans for a wild celebration.
He mailed coconut invitations to all,
and soon the whole town would be having a ball.

The jungle bash happened that Saturday night.
They all danced around in the glowing torchlight.
The limbo dance contest was truly amazing
as Jerry grabbed hold of a pole set a-blazing.

But the party soon went from the best to the worst
when the mayor's grass hula skirt suddenly burst
into flickering flames that flared from his fanny,
then spread through the jungle to each nook and cranny!

So the panicky crowd beat a hasty retreat
to escape from the jungle gym's horrible heat.
Jerry heard screams as the fire climbed higher—
Judy was trapped in the sky, in a tire!

Up in the air, very high overhead,
Judy hung on for dear life by a thread!
Now Jerry was certain she'd fall any minute.
If he was to save her, he'd better begin it.

He rescued her on his giraffe elevator.
"You're king of the jungle!" he yelled to persuade her.
As Judy snapped out of her terrified trance,
she barely escaped by the seat of her pants!

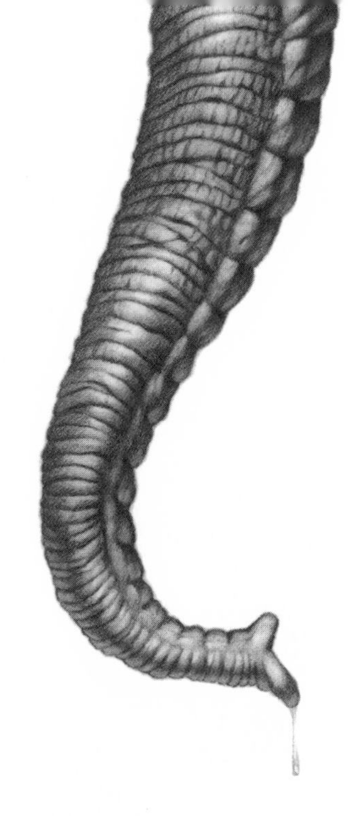

Then Jerry took charge of an army of elephants.
He battled the fire with courage and confidence.
The flames were no match for the streams from their noses.
They put out that blaze with their wrinkly gray hoses.

And everyone there learned a lesson that night,
that courage means acting in spite of your fright.
For Jerry had not only just saved the day,
he'd chased all his jungle gym jitters away.